DINOSAUR RESCUE

KYLE MEWBURN & DONOVAN BIXLEY

DAKO-SNAPPYSAURUS

SCHOLASTIC

AUCKLAND SYDNEY NEW YORK LONDON TORONTO
MEXICO CITY NEW DELHI HONG KONG BUENOS AIRES

Arg's Valley

1. Pterosaur Cliffs
2. Lava Mountain
3. Bog
4. Slimepot Swamp
5. Big Bone Lake
6. To the hunting grounds
7. Village Fire Pit
8. Arg's Village
9. Stinkooze Pit

Old Drik

Shlok
Arg's best friend

Arg
Caveboy genius

Krrk-Krrk
Arg's pet
Microceratops

Hng
Arg's big sister

Arg's mother

Arg's father

The author would like to point out he doesn't really believe Neanderthals and dinosaurs lived at the same time. He certainly didn't see any dinosaurs when he visited the Stone Age in his time machine while researching this book.

First published in 2012 by Scholastic New Zealand Limited
Private Bag 94407, Botany, Auckland 2163, New Zealand

Scholastic Australia Pty Limited
PO Box 579, Gosford, NSW 2250, Australia

Text © Kyle Mewburn, 2012
Illustrations © Donovan Bixley, 2012

ISBN 978-1-77543-098-8

National Library of New Zealand Cataloguing-in-Publication Data

Mewburn, Kyle.
Dako-snappysaurus / by Kyle Mewburn ; illustrated by Donovan Bixley.
(Dinosaur rescue ; bk. 6)
ISBN 978-1-77543-098-8
[1. Neanderthals—Fiction. 2. Dinosaurs—Fiction.] I. Bixley, Donovan.
II. Title. III. Mewburn, Kyle. Dinosaur rescue ; bk. 6.
NZ823.2—dc 23

12 11 10 9 8 7 6 5 4 3 2 1   2 3 4 5 6 7 8 9 / 1

Publishing team: Diana Murray, Penny Scown and Frith Hughes
Design and layup by Donovan Bixley
Typeset in Berkeley Oldstyle
Printed in China by RR Donnelley

Scholastic New Zealand's policy, in association with RR Donnelley, is to use papers that are renewable and made efficiently from wood grown in sustainable forests, so as to minimise its environmental footprint.

For Priscilla, who would rock even in the Stone Age – K.M.

For Malcolm and Hunter, a father/son hunting party – D.B.

CHAPTER ONE

Arg stormed to the far corner of his cave. He snatched up his special scratching stone and gouged a deep groove in the wall. Then he stepped back with a loud huff.

The wall was full of scratches. It looked like a sabre-tooth tiger had been sharpening its claws. But they weren't sabre-tooth tiger marks. They were counting marks. Each day Arg made a new mark. Every full moon, he scratched a circle above the mark. Each time something important happened, he scratched a different sign.

By counting his marks, and reading his signs, he could tell how long ago things had happened. Like it was three moons since the bungle nut trees flowered.

It was two moons ago when he and his dad got banned from the village because they got covered in stinkooze. He'd met his T-rex friend, Skeet, over six moons ago. And *eight* summers had passed since he was born. NOT seven!

Which meant he *was* old enough to join his dad on the hunting trip. If only his mum would believe him.

Arg had tried to convince her. But she didn't understand what Arg's scratches meant. And she couldn't count past three.

"Arg baby. No hunt," she would grunt. And that was that.

Shlok was nine moons younger than Arg. And *he* was going.

bubba bubba widdle Argy Wargy

It was so unfair. That's why Arg was so angry. Sometimes it was hard having a bigger brain than everyone else.

Arg sagged to the floor with a sigh. He could hear the hunting party getting ready to leave outside. There was a lot of cheering and crying and wailing and grunting going on. It was always an exciting and scary time for the tribe.

A successful hunt meant the tribe would have enough meat to eat for two moons. If it wasn't successful, everyone would have to eat roots and berries until the next hunt.

Several hunters probably wouldn't make it back home, either. They might get munched by a T-rex, or fall into a volcano, or, worst of all, get captured by the Grogllgrox. While the hunters were gone, the village was left unprotected, too.

Krrk-Krrk weaved in and out of Arg's feet, yapping wildly. He didn't like cheering ... or crying ... or any loud noise, really. He was such a scaredy-saur.

Krrk-Krrk
A real scaredy-saur

1. Krrk-Krrk is a *Microceratops*, meaning 'small horned'
2. Krrk-Krrk also has a defensive neck frill, which is handy as other dinosaurs and cave people frequently try to eat him!
3. Drool. There is always plenty of this around when Krrk-Krrk is hungry – which is ALL the time!
4. Defensive boney plates run down Krrk-Krrk's back to his tail, which is always wagging (unless he is running away)
5. Fat little tummy and stubby legs from eating too much meat and not getting any exercise (Microceratops are usually herbivores but Krrk-Krrk has grown fond of meat scraps)

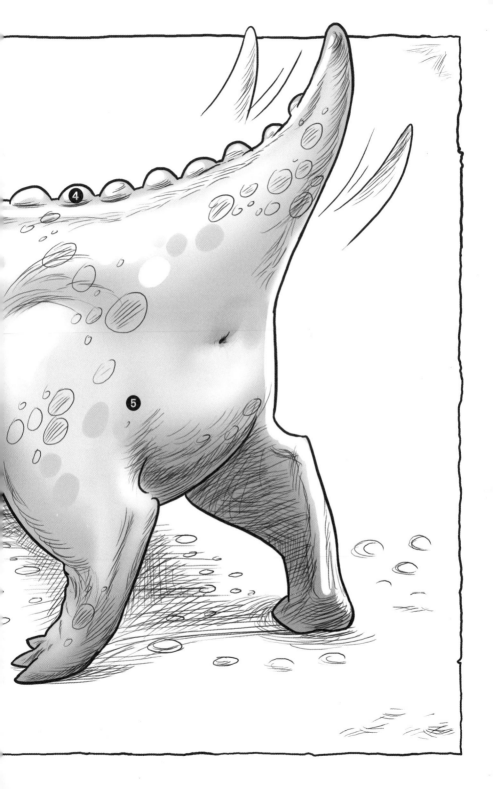

Arg scraped his scratching stone roughly along the ground. It sliced through the rock as easily as his dad's skinning stone cut through a cave bear's belly. Arg's stone was shiny and smooth and the colour of dinosaur teeth.

That's why when Arg first saw it lying in the sand beside the lake in the secret valley, he thought it WAS a dinosaur tooth. It wasn't the first time he'd made *that* mistake. Like the time he thought he'd found the tooth of a rare sabre-toothed tiger.

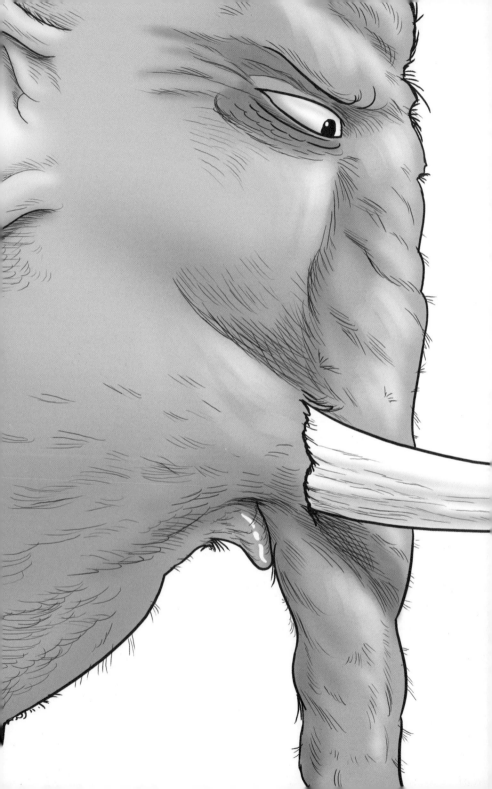

But when he tried to wrestle it loose, he discovered it was actually the tip of a mastodon tusk …

But that's another story.

Arg's Tooth Collection

T-rex teeth
are serrated down the
back edge and can be
used for sawing bones

Plateosaurus teeth
are very strange,
especially for a herbivore.
They would make good
arrowheads if only
Neanderthal's knew
what an arrow was!

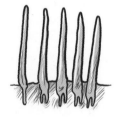

Hadrosaur teeth
are interlocking plates that
are excellent for scraping dried
stinkooze off your backside

Diplodocus teeth
are perfect for combs,
except that Neanderthals
don't comb their hair

Arg had the biggest collection of dinosaur teeth in the valley. Actually, it was the *only* collection of anything anywhere. Nobody else was interested in collecting things. Shlok did try collecting weird-looking beetles once. But he kept getting hungry and eating them.

When Arg realised it was just a stone, he was very disappointed. He slammed it against a nearby boulder, expecting it to be smashed to smithereens. He was very surprised when the boulder cracked instead!

The stone was very hard. Much, MUCH harder than normal valley stones. Skeet didn't know where the stone had come from. He'd never seen a stone like it before. It was like it had fallen out of the sky.

It had taken Arg ages to chip one end to a sharp point. The chips were very sharp, too. They made the best spearheads ever.

"Fat lot of good that is, if Mum won't even let me hunt," Arg muttered. "Stupid Neanderthals … *mutter … grumble … gripe …*"

Arg was so busy muttering under his breath, he didn't notice Krrk-Krrk snuffling away. By the time Arg glanced up, Krrk-Krrk had nearly reached the cave entrance. He wasn't just wandering off though. He was trying to catch a piece of meat, which was

tied to a long string. Each time Krrk-Krrk leapt at it, the meat was yanked away.

When Arg finally realised what was happening, it was nearly too late.

"Krrk-Krrk! Stop!" yelled Arg as he leapt to his feet.

Krrk-Krrk gave an annoyed yap, then chased after the meat. He never listened to Arg when he was chasing food. There was no time to lose.

Arg sprinted across the cave and dived. He
snatched up Krrk-Krrk and slid through the entrance
in a cloud of dust.

Just as Arg suspected, his sister Hng was
crouching on the other side. She was holding the
end of the string in one hand … and a heavy club
in the other hand. When she saw Arg, she smiled.
It wasn't a very nice smile.

Arg's eyes sprang wide in fear. He was completely
defenceless. Hng had been trying to eat Krrk-Krrk
for ages. She wouldn't mind at all if Arg's head
accidentally got in the way.

Hng raised her club higher …

Suddenly a huge shadow blocked the cave entrance. Arg was very relieved to see his dad. His dad didn't say anything, just stood there scratching under his arm. He didn't understand what Hng and Arg were doing. It looked like a very dangerous game. But brothers and sisters liked playing dangerous games together, didn't they?

Finally Arg's dad shrugged.

"Arg come hunt," he grunted. He grabbed Arg by the collar and hoisted him to his feet.

Arg scuttled away, leaving Hng scowling evilly behind him.

A short history of time

Nobody actually invented time. It has always been around. So when people say they have no time, it's not true.

Even though Stone Age people didn't know anything about time, they kind of knew time was passing. The sun and moon moved across the sky. Day turned into night. Seasons passed. Glaciers crept down valleys then crept back up again. People were born, grew up and got eaten. If they didn't get eaten, they got old, then died. Most Stone Age people didn't live very long. Which is lucky because Retirement Homes hadn't been invented yet.

An old Neanderthal couple in their mid-30s who have begun to think about retirement

It's also lucky Stone Age people didn't have to go to school or work, because they would always have been late. It would have been very annoying trying to organise a meeting. You couldn't agree to meet at nine o'clock, because Stone Age people couldn't count to nine, and clocks hadn't been invented yet.

People have tried all sorts of ways to measure time accurately. The shadow of the sun. Dripping water. Falling sand. A swinging weight. These days, time is measured precisely by the speed of electrons in a caesium atom. (That's why some people say "Caesium the day!") Since most people don't own a caesium atom, they buy expensive watches instead.

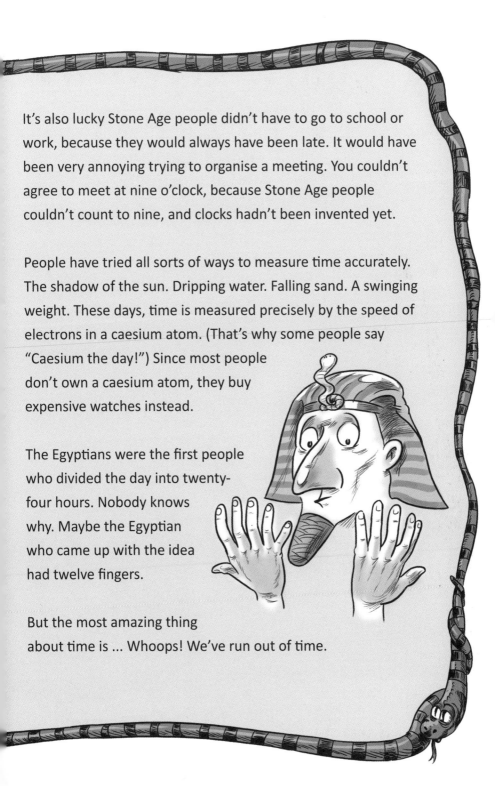

The Egyptians were the first people who divided the day into twenty-four hours. Nobody knows why. Maybe the Egyptian who came up with the idea had twelve fingers.

But the most amazing thing about time is ... Whoops! We've run out of time.

CHAPTER TWO

Arg raced around his cave in a whirlwind of excitement. He was going on his first hunting trip! He grabbed his spears and his club and his slingshot and some ammunition stones and some extra spearheads and ...

CRASH! CLATTER! *CLANG!*

Everything slipped from Arg's grasp and clattered to the floor. Arg scowled at the pile. There was just no way he could carry everything. He needed something to put it all in. But what?

His eyes swept around his cave.

Aha! That was it!

He hurried over to his bed rock and swept his cave-bear blanket onto the floor. Underneath was a mammoth stomach filled with Arg's breath. Both ends of the stomach were knotted so his breaths wouldn't escape. Arg called his invention a mamtress. He didn't think it sounded quite right, but he couldn't think of a better name yet.

The mamtress was covered in dried blood and bits of mammoth. It stank a bit, but it made his bed a lot softer to sleep on. Stone was very hard.

Arg quickly untied one end of the stomach.

Phhhhhhhhhhhtttttt! The breaths escaped in a loud, farting sound that filled the cave with putrid air.

Arg held his breath and yanked the stomach wide open. There was more than enough room inside for all his stuff. So he added an extra coat, his puckets and some hollow bones filled with his mum's special blood-stopping paste. It could be useful on a hunting trip.

Hmmm, was there anything else he might need? Should he take his set of different-coloured dinosaur poo in case he felt like painting something? Definitely. What about his cave-bear blanket? Well, it *could* get cold at night, couldn't it? And his special scratching stone? Why not. It was only a small stone. It wouldn't take up much room.

By the time Arg had finished packing, the stomach was way too heavy to lift. It took all Arg's strength just to drag it outside.

Everyone pointed and laughed when they saw Arg sweating and straining towards them. Even Shlok laughed. Arg's face turned red as a baboon's bum as he realised all the other hunters were just taking two spears. Nothing else.

Arg felt like crying and running back to his cave. But if he did that, he might never be able to go hunting. Then he'd have to go gathering food with the girls instead. That would be so embarrassing.

Arg gritted his teeth and dragged his bulging stomach towards the hunting party. He pretended not to notice everyone was making fun of him.

Halfway there the stomach sack was jerked roughly from his grasp. With a shout of protest, Arg tried to snatch it back ... then halted with a sheepish grin. Nobody was trying to take his stuff. It was just his dad trying to help.

"Thanks, Dad," said Arg.

His dad grunted. Arg couldn't tell if his dad was annoyed or embarrassed or something else. It was always hard to know what his dad was thinking. Maybe he wasn't thinking anything at all.

Arg's dad swung the bulging mammoth stomach over his shoulder as if it were full of pterosaur feathers instead of Arg's heavy stuff. Then he marched away without a word. He didn't join the others, but strode across the clearing and disappeared into the jungle. The rest of the hunting party grabbed their spears and set off in pursuit.

As Arg hurried to catch them, Krrk-Krrk came yapping at his heels.

"Sorry, Krrk-Krrk," said Arg. "It's too dangerous for you to come along. You'll have to stay here."

Krrk-Krrk didn't listen. He stayed close to Arg's feet. Sometimes microceratops could be very stubborn. Arg halted. He started to shoo Krrk-Krrk away ...

Then he saw Hng standing at the cave entrance. She wasn't watching the hunters leave. She was staring at Krrk-Krrk.

When Hng finally noticed that Arg was looking at her, she swung her club like she was smashing something. Then she licked her lips. Arg knew exactly what Hng was thinking.

He let out an enormous sigh. It would be very dangerous (not to mention embarrassing) to take Krrk-Krrk on the hunt with him. But it would be even more dangerous to leave him alone with Hng.

"Come on, then," said Arg.

Some Stone Age weapons that didn't catch on

People have always liked making weapons. In fact, the only thing people like more than *making* weapons is *using* weapons. The first weapons were stones and branches. They were useful for banging each other over the head, but not so useful if you were trying to stop a charging Triceratops. Then someone discovered that *sharp* stones and *pointy* sticks were much more effective.

People have been making bigger and better and more lethal weapons ever since. Every time someone invented a new weapon that was much better than everyone else's weapons, they tried to take over the whole world. They didn't stop until someone invented an even better weapon. Now there are weapons powerful enough to blow up the world. Stone Age people were always inventing new weapons too. Some weren't so useful.

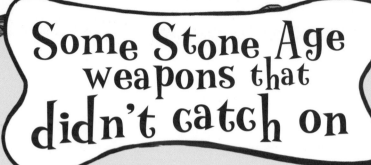

Bone and arrow *Idea*: if a length of rubbery sabre-tooth tiger intestine is knotted to each end of a mastodon thighbone, it can be used to fire sharpened sticks at an enemy. *Problem:* bones are not very bendy, so the stick didn't fly far. Bones are also very tasty. It was hard to stop people eating your bone. And even harder to stop wolves sneaking into the village and burying them.

Poomerang *Idea*: If a brontosaurus poo is carved into a crescent, it not only flies a lot further, it can knock your enemy's head off. (Dry brontosaurus poo is very hard.) *Problem:* If it *didn't* knock your enemy's head off, your enemy thought it was a gift. (Brontosaurus poo is very useful.) Instead of fighting, they wanted to be your friend. Worst of all, the poomerang sometimes came back!

Lavapult *Idea:* If a small tree is bent over and a chunk of lava is placed on the end, when the tree is released, the lava will be sent sailing towards your enemy. *Problem:* Lava is very hot. If it doesn't burn your hands off, it will burn the tree. It is also very hard to aim. Even if you *do* manage to fire it, it usually goes straight up in the air ... or into your neighbour's cave.

CHAPTER THREE

When the hunting party set off, everyone was laughing and grunting with happiness. They all felt like singing ... or they would have, except songs hadn't been invented yet. Hunting was like an exciting game. If everything went well, they'd soon be feasting on allosaurus steaks or oviraptor kebabs.

But as the jungle closed in around them, they started thinking about what might happen if everything *didn't* go well. They could get gobbled by a spinosaur, snatched by a pterosaur, attacked by a Grogllgrox, strangled by a giant snake, stung by a poisonous spider or devoured by a man-eating plant. They could easily slip down a glacier, fall into a crevasse, be boiled alive in a geyser, get buried under an avalanche or drown in a quicksand pit.

They might get lost, or sick, or poison themselves by eating the wrong berries, or ...

Well, there were way too many terrible things that could happen.

By the time they reached the end of the valley, everyone was getting jumpy. The jungle was dark and unfamiliar. They rarely came this way. If Arg's

dad hadn't been marching bravely ahead, they might have all turned around and scurried back home.

The path was only wide enough for one person. The hunters were strung out in a long line and kept their eyes and ears peeled. Anything could be hiding in the jungle, waiting to pounce.

Arg was walking in the middle of the line. He would have loved to walk beside his dad, but every time he tried to catch up, his dad walked faster. Arg wasn't sure if his dad was angry, or if he was just trying to protect Arg. The front and back of the line were the most dangerous positions.

Krrk-Krrk kept very close by Arg's feet. He hadn't made a sound since they'd left the village.

Arg's tongue was bitter and dry. It tasted like he'd been sucking a dragonfly. He'd thought hunting would be good fun. Now he wasn't so sure. Maybe it wouldn't have been so bad to go gathering food with the girls. Better to be laughed at than to be eaten by a spinosaur.

S-C-R-E-E-E-E-E-E-C-H!

The megaraptor sounded close. Terrifyingly close. So close, in fact, that as Arg spun round to face it, he wasn't sure he'd make it in time. Any second he was going to be chomped in half. And his whizzing brain's last thought would be – how did a mega-raptor get so close without anyone hearing it? If megaraptors had learnt how to be *that* sneaky, people were going to be in serious trouble.

Arg threw up his arms. His heart was pounding so hard his spear shook in his hands. He opened his mouth to let out a fierce cry. If he was going to die, he was going to die like a warrior. But all that came out was a strangled gasp.

Arg's head whipped one way, then the other. But there was no sign of the megaraptor. Huh? It didn't make any sense.

Then Shlok started laughing.

"Shlok scare Arg! Shlok scare ..."

A hail of spears came whizzing through the air
from every direction. One almost pierced Arg's ear as
he threw himself onto the ground. He covered his
head with his hands and squeezed his eyes tightly
closed.

Shlok didn't move. His brain was too slow to figure out what was happening. He was going to be killed!

THONK!

THONK!

THONK!

THONK!

THONK!

The spears whooshed past Shlok's head and stuck into a cycad. Shlok stood grinning and picking his nose. He didn't realise he'd been a whisker away from being speared. He thought it was a funny game. It was lucky the hunters weren't better shots.

"Shlok scare Arg!" grunted Shlok.

As Arg dusted himself off, he shook his head. There were two more things to add to his list of things that could go wrong. Getting accidentally speared by jumpy hunters. And getting killed by one of Shlok's practical jokes.

Shlok's practical jokes

WARNING! Do not try these jokes on your friends.
Shlok is a professionally trained Neanderthal.

The hunters started to relax as soon as they reached the next valley. Apart from small patches of jungle along the edges, it was all open grassland. There was nowhere a man-eating dinosaur could be hiding. And if any predator tried to sneak up on them, the brontosauruses would soon sound an alarm. With their long necks, brontosauruses were great lookouts.

Krrk-Krrk was a lot more relaxed, too. He strutted ahead of Arg like he was a T-rex instead of a scaredy-saur microceratops. He strayed further and further away, until he disappeared completely from view. Arg slowly counted his breaths. If he got to ten without hearing a sound, he'd start to worry. One ... two ...

Krrk-Krrk burst out of the long grass with a chatter of fearful yelps. He raced to Arg and hid behind his feet. Arg gripped his spear tightly as he heard something rustling closer. There could be all sorts of dangerous creatures hiding in the grass. Snakes and scorpions and ...

Sniff
Sniff

When a giant dung beetle slowly waddled onto
the path, Arg could only roll his eyes. Who could be
afraid of a dung beetle?

Shlok wasn't afraid. He was hungry. He licked his
lips and snatched up the beetle. It squirmed and
wriggled, but it couldn't escape. Shlok chomped off
its head and spat it onto the ground. Brown slime
oozed down Shlok's chin as he sucked out the
beetle's juices.

Arg's stomach churned in disgust. Shlok was such
a ... such a ...

Arg sighed. He couldn't
think of an animal who
ate like Shlok, because
pigs hadn't been
invented yet.

Suddenly, the hunters halted. At the front of the line, Arg's dad sniffed the air while the others waited patiently behind. Arg copied his dad, trying to figure out what scents might be carried on the wind. But all he could smell were stale brontosaurus farts.

Everywhere Arg looked, brontosauruses were grazing the tall grass. He'd never seen so many brontosauruses in one place before. The rumble of brontosaurus farts echoed off the hills like an avalanche.

But they weren't there to hunt brontosaurus.

A huge grin swept over Arg's dad's face. He gave an excited cry, then headed towards a dark crack in the valley wall.

CHAPTER FOUR

Inside the crack, it was dark and damp. Arg could just see Shlok's outline ahead of him. The path was littered with jagged rocks that tugged and tore at Arg's coat. Drops of icy water dribbled down his neck.

Everything smelt strange. Kind of like his dad when he ran around on a very hot day.

Even the sounds were strange. It sounded like a spinosaurus snoring through a nose full of snot. Arg couldn't imagine where they were headed. He just had to trust that his dad knew what he was doing.

Slowly, the crack opened wider. With every step, the snoring sound got louder and louder.

When they finally stumbled into the sunshine, Arg's eyes sprang open. They were standing beside a vast lake. It stretched all the way to the horizon. It wasn't like any lake Arg had ever seen. Huge waves crashed onto the rocks, churning the water into sand and foam. Even the rocks were different. They weren't coated with moss like normal lake rocks. They were covered by thousands of weird, knobbly lumps.

The hunters hurried over to the rocks and started smashing them with heavy stones. After a few hefty bashes, the knobbly lumps burst open. Inside were greyish, slithery blobs as big as Arg's head. It looked like the stuff inside eyeballs. Arg couldn't believe his eyes when the hunters started

eating them! He couldn't even tell if it was animal, vegetable or something else completely.

Shlok quickly joined in the feast. He didn't care what it was as long as it was edible. Krrk-Krrk ran between the men, slurping up any bits that fell to the ground.

When Arg's dad realised Arg wasn't gorging himself too, he fished out a huge blob and offered it to Arg.

"Mmmmm, good," grunted Arg's dad. "Arg eat,"

"Thanks, Dad, but I'm not really hungry. I think I'll wait until dinner." Arg tried not to gag as his dad noisily slurped and chewed the blob into pieces. He wished his dad would close his mouth when he was eating. He was such a Neanderthal sometimes.

Delicious Neanderthal Foods

Pretzel-co-atlus
For a great snack when
you're on the fly

Diplodocustard
Yellow and gooey
(you don't want to know
where this comes from!)

Barbec-utah-raptor
You'll be rapt with
this traditional taste
of outdoor cooking

Scrambled steggs
Mushed up stegosaurus eggs, just the way your great-great-great-great-great-great- (you get the idea) great-grandmother used to make them

Pie-ceratops
Like a potato-top pie but now with added triceratops!

Thai-rannosaurus
With a touch of chilli, this is a spicy alternative to your T-mex burrito

Arg's stomach gurgled in protest. He certainly hoped they caught something more edible before nightfall. Or at least something recognisable.

One by one the hunters finished gorging themselves. They collapsed onto the sand with their hands on their bloated bellies and satisfied smiles on their faces. Krrk-Krrk was lying on his back with his feet in the air and his tongue hanging out. If his tail wasn't wagging, Arg might have thought he was dead.

Arg sat on a nearby rock, yawning. He never imagined a hunting trip could be SO boring. And he knew that as long as there was plenty of easy food around, the hunters wouldn't bother trying to catch anything else. Neanderthals were incredibly lazy. But Arg would rather starve than eat one of those rock blobs.

Arg's stomach grumbled loudly in protest. He was getting hungrier every breath. Shielding his eyes, he scanned the beach. Nothing.

He let his gaze skim across the lake. Still nothing.

He gazed up at the sky. Empty ... except that one cloud looked a bit like a yummy oviraptor, and another one could be a roasted iguanodon leg and ...

With an enormous sigh, Arg got to his feet. If he didn't eat something soon, he'd faint. He was determined not to let that happen. His dad was

probably embarrassed enough carrying all Arg's stuff. There was no way he was going to make his dad carry him, too.

Arg marched over to the knobbly rock as if he were about to battle a cave bear. He wished he was about to battle a cave bear. It would be a lot easier than eating a rock blob. He couldn't understand why his dad had led them to such an empty beach.

Arg's dad let out a loud groan.

Serves yourself right for eating so many rock blobs, thought Arg. If they hadn't all gorged themselves, they could be sitting around a fire roasting lovely fresh fish or something by now.

He grabbed a heavy stone and smashed it against the smallest lump he could find. It opened with a satisfying crack. Arg fished out a slithery, slimy blob and sniffed it carefully. It smelt like Old Drik's armpits.

Arg's dad let out another groan as Arg licked the blob. "Urrrrggghh!" spat Arg. His face crinkled with disgust. He'd rather lick Old Drik's armpits than eat a single blob. His eyes scoured the beach again. There had to be *something* else he could eat. Some algae, maybe. Or a rotting jellyfish. Anything! But there was just rocks and sand.

By now all the other hunters had started groaning loudly, too. Shlok's tongue was flopping out of his mouth. Foamy drool dribbled down his chin.

Boy, they really must have stuffed themselves, thought Arg.

He tilted back his head and dangled the blob just above his mouth. If he could manage to eat just one, he'd have enough energy to go search for something better.

The groaning got louder.

Arg closed his eyes. Stagnant water dribbled onto his tongue. His whole face crinkled as he lowered the blob into his mouth. His teeth chomped together. It spurted liquid that tasted like pus. But he kept chewing.

All he had to do now was swallow.

On the count of three. One ... two ...

When Krrk-Krrk let out a strange yelping whine, Arg's eyes sprang open. He'd never heard Krrk-Krrk make that noise before.

Krrk-Krrk was lying on his side with his head in a pool of microceratops vomit. Arg frowned. Krrk-Krrk was never sick.

Arg's dad suddenly bolted upright in a geyser of vomit.
It drenched his legs and sprayed the other hunters.

As he wiped vomit off his chin, he saw Arg
watching him. Arg's mouth was hanging open.
The half-chewed rock-blob was still balanced on
his tongue.

Arg's dad gave him a sheepish smile. "Arg ...

BLUUUUURRRRGGGGHHHH!!!

He fell back with a pained groan. His hands
gripped his stomach.

Arg spat out the rock-blob and ran to the lake. He
slurped up a mouthful of water and swished it round
in his mouth. The water tasted like salty fish.

Behind him, the other hunters started vomiting violently. The vomit was runny and flecked with rubbery chunks of rock-blob. By the time Arg had rinsed out his mouth, the beach was drenched in vomit. So were the hunters. The beach echoed with loud groans. It sounded as though they were all dying.

A cold shiver ran up Arg's hairy spine. If the hunters died, he'd be stranded there all alone. He didn't even know how to get home! And if his dad died ...

NO! He wasn't even going to think about that.

"A-r-r-r-r-g ..." Arg's dad called his name. But it was so quiet it was nearly drowned out by the waves. "A-r-r-r-r-g ..."

Arg hurried to his dad's side. His dad's chin was speckled with vomit. Dried spit was sticking to the corners of his mouth. And he was shivering like he was lying on a glacier instead of a warm, sandy beach. That was the scariest bit.

"W-a-a-a-a-a-a-t-e-r," whispered Arg's dad. His dry tongue scraped across vomity lips.

Arg's jaw clenched with determination. His dad and Krrk-Krrk and Shlok and everyone else were relying on him. He wouldn't let them down.

All the hunters were groaning for water. The lake water was too salty but there was plenty of water trickling down the cliffs. It would take forever to carry water in his cupped hands. He needed something bigger. But what?

Aha! An empty trilobite shell was swept onto the beach by a wave. Before the next wave could whisk it

68

away, Arg snatched it up. He filled it to the brim, then hurried back to his dad. He trickled the water into his dad's mouth and was relieved when he smiled weakly.

Backwards and forwards Arg ran. By the time everyone had slurped their share, most of the hunters had fallen into a light, shivering sleep. It was still warm, but Arg could already feel night's cold breath on his neck. If he didn't get a fire going soon, they could freeze to death. A fire was the only way to keep prowling night creatures away, too.

Arg gathered up bits of driftwood and dried grass and leaves. Then he fished out his dad's flintstone. He'd never made a fire before. But he'd watched his dad heaps of times. A few quick flicks sent sparks flying into the grass. It smouldered and smoked until Arg blew it carefully alight.

He stoked the fire until it crackled and roared. His stomach grumbled noisily, but he ignored it. There was nothing to eat, and the shadows were already reaching across the beach. It would soon be dark. There was no way Arg was going to venture far from the safety of the fire.

Arg's dad rolled over with a groan. It couldn't be very comfortable lying on the cold, hard sand.

Arg emptied the mammoth stomach and slowly re-filled it with breath. He dragged and wrestled his dad onto the stomach then covered him with the cave-bear blanket. His dad let out a long sigh. Arg slipped Krrk-Krrk under the blanket beside his dad, then grabbed his spear.

He found a good lookout spot on the edge of the fire's circle of light. Someone had to stand guard. It was going to be a long night.

Fire: a burning issue

Fire is amazing stuff. It can keep you warm, cook your dinner, fight off enemies and scare away nasties. In fact, it's just like your mum. Except you shouldn't try to kiss or hug a fire. And fires are no good at tucking you into bed or reading bedtime stories.

Even the smoke from fires is useful. It can preserve food, send messages, smoke out bandits or calm bees. Really, the only thing more useful than fire is water.

LUCKY!

KAZZZZAAP

Most animals are terrified of fire. People were probably scared, too, until they discovered how useful it was. Stone Age people made fires by dipping branches in lava, then carrying the burning branch back to their cave. Or waiting for lightning to strike nearby.

But it could be a long walk to the nearest lava. And lightning didn't always strike when you needed it. Luckily they discovered it was easy to make their own fire by making sparks with a flintstone, or spinning a thin stick very fast between their hands until it got hot enough to set grass alight.

Sometimes the fire set everything alight. That's why people invented fire brigades. The first fire brigade was invented in Rome by Marcus Crassus. It wasn't a very nice fire brigade. If a building was burning, they would rush to the scene. But they wouldn't try to put the fire out until the owners paid them. Today they wouldn't be called a fire brigade, they'd be called the Mafia.

Without fire, we wouldn't be able to fire someone. Or fire a cannon. Or fire someone out of a cannon. We couldn't make toast or roast marshmallows. We couldn't tell spooky stories around a campfire or hang stockings around a fireplace at Christmas. Which means neither Boy Scouts nor Santa Claus would have been invented. Without Boy Scouts, old ladies could never cross the road. And without Santa, reindeer would be running wild everywhere.

You're fired!

CHAPTER FIVE

Arg's eyes blinked open. The sun was shining warmly in his face. He must have fallen asleep. He smiled as he stretched into a lazy yawn. It was morning and he was still alive!

The others had survived, too. Their groans had been replaced by loud snores. They didn't sound as if they were going to die any more. Everything was going to be fine.

Arg's stomach grumbled noisily. *Everything will be fine as long as I can find something to eat soon,* Arg corrected himself.

He jumped to his feet, grabbed his spear ... then froze. His mouth gaped open. Before he'd fallen asleep, everyone had been curled up around the fire. Now they were all scattered and tumbled across the beach. And the fire was gone! It looked like a herd of spinosaurs had snuck into the camp during the night and played catch with the hunters.

Make that a herd of very *wet* spinosaurs. The hunters were drenched and the sand was damp. If Arg didn't know better, he would have thought the lake had crept up the beach during the night and washed away their camp. But lakes couldn't grow ... could they?

Arg glimpsed a fleck of white in the sand. His special scratching stone! As he snatched it up, he saw the tip of his slingshot. He dropped to his knees and started sifting frantically through the sand.

All his stuff!

He found three of his coloured poos, one of his mum's blood-stopping pastes and ...

Then he remembered his mamtress. (Okay, so Arg might have a big brain, but big brains don't always

work properly. Or quickly.)

He jerked upright. His head whipped left. Then right. There was no sign of his mamtress. And no sign of Krrk-Krrk or his dad either!

"Dad! Krrk-Krrk!" yelled Arg as he sprinted along the beach. "Dad! Krr–"

A flicker of movement caught his eye. There was something floating on the lake. Something big and lumpy and sort of mamtress-shaped.

An arm lifted weakly and waved. It was definitely Arg's dad. The wind was blowing him further away with every breath. Arg had to do something. And fast.

Arg was a good swimmer. If he took his time, he was sure he'd make it. Even with a grumbling, empty stomach. He took off his coat and waded into the water. It only took a few steps before he realised why his dad had brought them here. The lake was teeming with fish. In no time they could spear enough to last the approaching cold season. Fish were easy to dry, and light to carry.

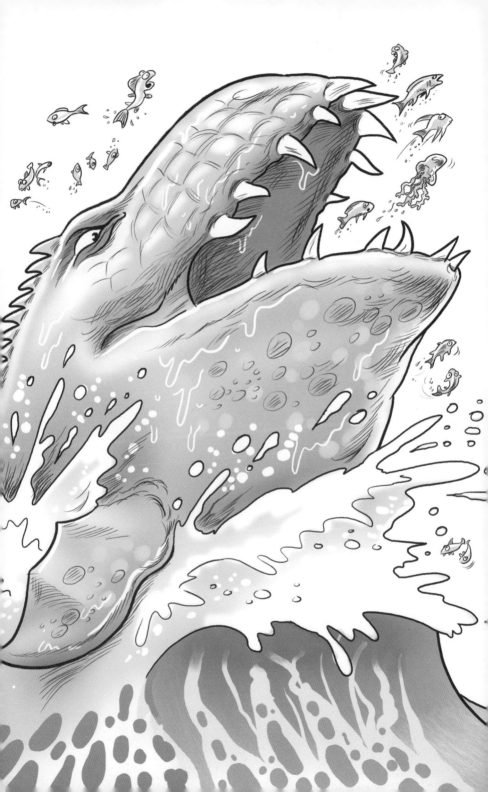

Suddenly, the lake began bubbling and frothing. Arg's head jerked up as a massive tail sliced through the surface. It was a dakosaurus! And it was heading straight for him!

Arg raced towards the shore.

The dakosaurus rose out of the water.

Arg threw himself onto the beach.

SNAP! SNAP! The dakosaurus plunged into the swirling mass of frantic fish and thrashed its powerful jaws. Chunks of scales and blood flew everywhere. A dozen fish vanished down its throat as it speared through the water. Then it submerged without a trace.

That was close, thought Arg. His heart was almost leaping out of his chest. There was no way he could swim out to his dad with a dakosaurus cruising nearby. The mamtress was drifting further and further away, too. Soon it would be out of reach.

Dakosaurus
the mouth with flippers

1. Dakosaurus (*tearing lizard*) was the original Jaws, with a huge head full of serrated teeth like an underwater T-rex. Dakosaurus was not actually a dinosaur; but was related to crocodiles
2. Four powerful flippers were remnants of legs of its land-dwelling ancestors
3. It's prey was pretty much everything in the sea including other large marine reptiles such as ichthyosaurs and plesiosaurs
4. Size compared to Arg
5. Long, crocodile-like tail with a rudder-like fin gave it powerful thrust for ambushing prey

Arg's throat filled with fear as the dakosaurus's tail broke the surface again. It wasn't prowling the shore any more. It had changed course and was heading straight for the mamtress. If Arg didn't act quickly, it would be too late.

Arg snatched up his slingshot. It was his only hope.

The dakosaurus began circling the mamtress, getting closer each time. At the end of each circle, it leapt out of the water and slashed the air with its jaws.

SNAP!

SNAP!

Arg scoured the beach, searching for one of his ammunition stones. But they'd all been swallowed by the sand. The stones that littered the beach were all too big or too knobbly for his slingshot. The only stone anywhere near the right size was Arg's special scratching stone. But he couldn't use that. He might never find another one.

SNAP! SNAP!

The dakosaurus made a wide, frothing circle, then veered straight towards the mamtress. Arg knew that this time it was going in for the kill. There was no time to lose. And no time to worry about stupid stones. Arg placed his scratching stone in his slingshot and pulled the cord back as far as it would go. He would have only

one chance. He couldn't afford to miss his target.

With a mighty thrashing of its tail, the dakosaurus rose out of the water. Its jaws opened wide. It was going to grab the mamtress and drag it under!

Arg took a deep breath. Carefully, he aimed ... then fired.

The stone flashed through the air like a meteor. It arced towards the dakosaurus ... then began to dip.

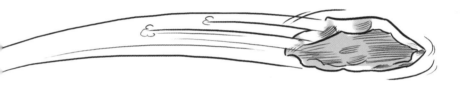

Arg's heart sank. The stone was going to fall just short. The stone hit the water a spear-throw from its target. But it didn't sink straight away. It skipped across the surface.

Arg grimaced. His shot was right on target, but that wasn't much use now. Even if it struck the dakosaurus, it wouldn't hurt it. His dad and Krrk-Krrk were goners. He couldn't bear to watch!

The stone clipped the edge of the mamtress.

Arg's breaths rushed out in a loud fart. The mamtress shot forward ...

The dakosaurus made its final lunge. **SNAP!** Its jaws snapped together, catching nothing but air and water. The mamtress skimmed along the lake, heading for shore.

The angry dakosaurus wasn't going to let its prey escape so easily. Its tail swept mightily, left and right, powering it through the water in pursuit.

Arg held his breath. The mamtress was slowing ... or the dakosaurus was gaining. It was going to be close!

swoooooosh!

The mamtress hit the beach and slid up onto the sand. It came to a stop in a last gasp of escaping air. But its passengers weren't safe yet. The dakosaurus burst out of the water and slid onto the sand. It thrashed its tail, writhing closer and closer.

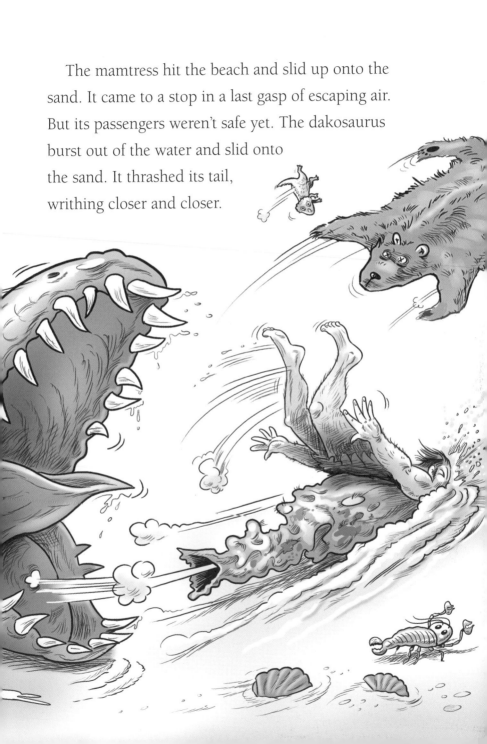

Arg raced across the sand and grabbed his spear. He dodged around the dakosaur's snapping jaws, then plunged his spear through the creature's eye. The dakosaurus thrashed once. A violent shudder rolled down its enormous body. Then it went still.

Arg was panting so strongly his whole body heaved. He felt as if he'd run a thousand steps up the steepest hill. He was a real hunter now. But he didn't feel excited or elated. He just felt exhausted and a little sad. Almost as deflated as the saggy mamtress.

When the hunters finally woke from their feverish sleep, they thought they were dreaming. For a start, they were all lying halfway up the beach, when they clearly remembered collapsing right beside the water ... or was that part of their dream too?

More surprising still, there was a roaring fire going. Only the most experienced hunters knew how to light a fire. But none of them could remember lighting it.

Even more surprising, there were long lines of fish drying in the sun. And a huge dakosaurus lying beside the lake, waiting to be carved into pieces.

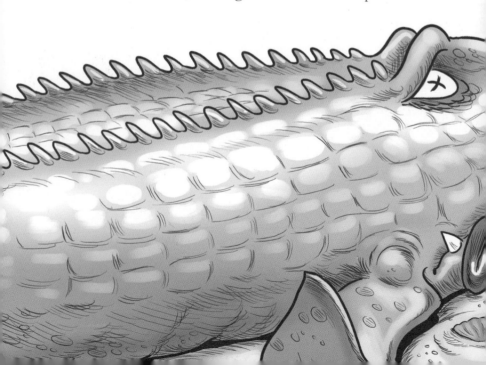

What great hunter had killed the dakosaurus?
It normally took an entire hunting party using their
cleverest tricks to snare a dakosaurus. And they were
lucky if someone didn't lose an arm or a leg or two.

But perhaps the biggest surprise of all was seeing
Arg, sitting by the fire, roasting fish. If they didn't
know better, they would have thought
Arg had done everything. But
Arg wasn't a hunter.
He was just a boy.

They scratched their heads and tried to think of another explanation. But their brains were way too small. Maybe they had done it, and just forgot.

"Mmmmm, fish," they all grunted.

As Arg shared the fish around, he noticed his dad watching him. When he finally glanced over, his dad smiled. It was a very proud smile and it made Arg beam with delight. They both knew who had killed the dakosaurus and lit the fire and everything else. And that was all that mattered.